This book is to be returned on or before the last date below.
You may renew the book unless it is requested by another borrower.
THANK YOU FOR USING YOUR LIBRARY

GREAT BARR
0121 357 1340

- 7 MAY 2013

D0186200

DOCTOR WHO

The Silurian Gift

DOCTOR WHO

The Silurian Gift

Mike Tucker

1 3 5 7 9 10 8 6 4 2

Published in 2013 by BBC Books, an imprint of Ebury Publishing
A Random House Group Company

Doctor Who is a BBC Wales production for BBC One.
Executive producers: Steven Moffat and Caroline Skinner

The Random House Group Limited Reg. No. 954009

Addresses for companies within the Random House Group can be found at
www.randomhouse.co.uk

A CIP catalogue record for this book is available from the British Library.

ISBN 978 1 849 90558 9

The Random House Group Limited supports The Forest Stewardship Council
(FSC®), the leading international forest certification organisation. Our books
carrying the FSC label are printed on FSC® certified paper. FSC is the only forest
certification scheme endorsed by the leading environmental organisations,
including Greenpeace. Our paper procurement policy can be found at
www.randomhouse.co.uk/environment

Editorial director: Albert DePetrillo
Editorial manager: Nicholas Payne
Series consultant: Justin Richards
Project editor: Steve Tribe
Cover design: Lee Binding © Woodlands Books Ltd, 2013
Production: Alex Goddard

Printed and bound by CPI Group (UK) Ltd, Croydon, CR0 4YY

To buy books by your favourite authors and register for offers,
visit www.randomhouse.co.uk

Chapter One

Bob Clamp was cold. Colder than he had ever been in his life. Given where he was, he really shouldn't have found his coldness quite so surprising. He crossed to the window of the small security hut and stared out at the falling snow.

'The South Pole,' he muttered. 'How on earth did I end up in Antarctica?'

There was an easy answer to that question. Work. Two months ago he had lost his job. He'd been a bouncer at a Croydon nightclub, but the club had been steadily losing money and customers, until everyone had been laid off. He tried to get another job in London, but there didn't seem to be anything about. Not for someone of his age, at any rate.

Then he saw the advert in the paper. Security guard for a top-secret project with PelCorp. That had made him think. He'd always fancied himself as a secret agent when he was younger. The idea of working on something 'top secret' was too good to miss.

To his surprise he got an interview straight away. It was with the boss of the company, a flash American named Rick Pelham.

Bob glanced at the newspaper on the table. Pelham's photo was all over the front page. He claimed he had the solution to the energy crisis. Bob snorted. If he'd known that this was the 'top-secret' project…

He peered at the rows of oil drums lined up outside in the snow. The PelCorp logo was on each one. It didn't look like much, but his new boss Pelham had said that this was the answer. Bob didn't understand how this 'Fire Ice' was going to put more petrol in people's cars, but Pelham was paying him very well to guard the drums. Not that he knew quite who he was guarding them from, mind you. He shook his head. 'As if anyone is going to trek all the way down here to steal barrels…'

Almost as soon as the words had left his lips, a strange electronic noise filled the air. Bob caught sight of a dark shape flitting through the snow flurries on the far side of the compound. Cursing under his breath, he snatched up his torch. He struggled with the zip on his coat, then pulled on his gloves and goggles and hurried out into the freezing night.

Flinching against the biting wind, Bob made his way over to where he thought he had seen the figure. Sure enough, there were footprints in the fresh snow.

The odd noise came again. He pulled the taser stun gun from his belt and peered into the swirling snow. 'All right, I know you're out here. There's no point in hiding.' He started to move through the lines of oil drums.

Suddenly a dark shape was caught in the light from his torch.

'OK. Come out. I'm warning you. I'm armed,' Bob called.

The shape darted to one side, and Bob caught a glimpse of shaggy fur. He backed off. He could deal with a man, but not with some kind of animal. He reached for the radio on his belt, intending to call his boss for back-up. As he did so, he became aware of a shadow falling over him, and of the sound of monstrous breathing.

Bob turned, looking up in disbelief as something huge loomed over him. The radio dropped from his gloved hands as he fumbled with his weapon. The monstrous thing gave a huge roar, then razor-sharp claws slashed down.

The strange electronic burble cut through

the air again and the huge shape turned and moved away. Silence settled over the ranks of oil drums once more as the snow started to turn a deep, dark red.

Laughter rang in Rick Pelham's ears. He glared in irritation at the strange young man in the tweed jacket and bow tie sitting in the front row of the meeting room.

The day had started out so well, Pelham thought. He had dressed in his most expensive suit, made sure that his stylist had made his hair look just right and had a cup of his favourite coffee.

He had watched as the journalists he had invited were flown in by helicopter. They had stumbled across the deck of the ship, shivering from the cold in their waterproof anoraks. Once in the meeting room, they had been left to wait, drinking lukewarm coffee from plastic cups. Rick Pelham knew how to make an entrance. By the time he appeared to make his announcement, they should have been glad to see him.

Instead he was being made to look foolish.

'Forgive me, Mister...?'

'Doctor, actually,' said the young man cheerfully.

'Doctor.' Pelham forced himself to smile. 'And which paper are you from, again?'

'Oh, the *Beezer*, I think.' The man waved his hands around airily. 'Or *Whizzer and Chips*... One of the quality tabloids.'

'Well, you have been asking rather a lot of questions. Perhaps if someone else could ask something...'

'Oh, they'll just ask you boring stuff, like what breakfast cereal you prefer or whether your hair is real,' said the Doctor. 'But there's something I want to know. Out of all the hundreds and hundreds of miles of ice and snow in Antarctica, how did you manage to find this great fire-ice-fuel-source thingy? And on your first try? Was it a lucky guess?'

Pelham tried to ignore the chuckles of the other journalists. 'It wasn't exactly luck, Doctor,' he said. 'We did a lot of research. Now that I am ready to deliver our first shipload of fuel to the world, it seems a good time to...'

'Yes, that's another thing,' interrupted the Doctor. 'Extracting and refining the actual fuel from the ice should have taken you years. You've managed it in a few weeks. Even I couldn't do it that fast!'

'Well, perhaps I'm cleverer than you,' said Pelham through gritted teeth.

The Doctor frowned. 'No, I don't think that can be true...'

There was another ripple of laughter from the room. Pelham could feel his temper starting to rise. 'Well if you will let me continue, perhaps I can prove that to you,' he said.

The Doctor leant back in his chair and folded his arms. 'Right-oh. Off you go then. Best of luck.'

Before Pelham could say another word, the ship's alarms went off. He glared at his personal assistant, Matt. 'What the devil is going on?'

Matt was struggling to listen to the message coming through his headset.

'It's the refinery, sir. There's been some kind of accident.' He looked shocked. 'Some kind of animal attack.'

Suddenly the man in the bow tie was there at Matt's shoulder. His face was grave. 'Then I think that we should get out there right away, don't you? I am a Doctor, after all.'

Chapter Two

The Doctor watched as sailors unlashed a helicopter from the deck of the tanker. He was worried. He'd been concerned before he had come out here. Pelham's discovery of a new super-fuel had been all over the newspapers, but it all seemed too good to be true. When he'd heard that there was to be a publicity launch he'd pulled some strings at UNIT (the Unified Intelligence Taskforce) to get out here. Now, with an attack on the refinery and a mystery animal on the loose, he was convinced that his hunch was correct. Something was very wrong.

Pelham's assistant, Matt, waved him over. 'If you're coming, you'd better hurry. There's a storm blowing in. We need to leave before it hits.'

As the Doctor started to cross the deck towards the waiting helicopter, a voice called out from behind him.

'Doctor, hang on a moment.'

The Doctor turned to see a young woman

hurrying towards him, a black briefcase in her arms. He frowned. She was one of the other journalists, wasn't she?

'You're so forgetful,' said the woman breathlessly. 'You left your case!'

The girl turned to Matt, hand outstretched. 'Lizzie Davies. Doctor's assistant. I'll be coming out too.'

Matt ignored the offered hand and bustled the two of them towards the helicopter. 'Yes, fine. Just hurry. Mr Pelham wants to get to the refinery as quickly as possible.'

The Doctor clambered into the aircraft. Pelham was in the pilot's seat. It seemed that there was no end to the man's talents. As the Doctor strapped himself into the seat next to Lizzie, he turned and raised an eyebrow at her. 'You're my assistant?'

Lizzie gave him a sly smile. 'For the moment, yes.' Her face fell. 'Unless you're going to give me away...'

'Not at all!' The Doctor beamed at her. 'I like you, Lizzie Davies. Clever, cheeky, just what I need on an adventure like this. I just hope you know what you're letting yourself in for.'

Lizzie tapped the case. 'With luck, some good photos for a quality tabloid newspaper!'

she whispered.

The Doctor grinned at her as the helicopter gave a throaty roar and lurched into the air.

The helicopter swept across the cold grey water of the Antarctic Ocean. The bulky shape of the cargo ship they had left was far behind them in moments. Matt kept up a constant sales pitch.

'Of course, Mr Pelham is also ensuring that a specially built fleet of PelCorp cargo ships will be on standby to deliver the Fire Ice across the planet. At present the refinery is still at an early stage, but as time goes on we aim to expand it.'

The Doctor stared out of the helicopter window as the refinery slowly came into view on the distant ice. It seemed to be nothing but a collection of metal shacks dumped down on the ice. A fenced area enclosed hundreds of barrels of Fire Ice, waiting to be shipped to the coast on snow tractors. In the distance a tall tower, the drilling rig, jutted up into a darkening sky.

'Doesn't look like much to me,' muttered Lizzie.

'Well, a lot of the labs and work rooms are under the ice,' explained Matt. 'The fuel itself is being mined from an underground lake.'

'Yes,' murmured the Doctor. 'It's being mined from an underground lake that has been untouched for millions of years.'

Matt bristled in anger. 'I can tell you that every care has been taken to ensure that we have as little impact on the environment as possible.'

The Doctor stared at him. 'But what steps have you taken to ensure that *it* has no impact on *you*?'

The helicopter landed heavily on the ice. Pelham and his passengers were bustled into the refinery. Pelham was quickly surrounded by dozens of assistants, all of them talking at once. For a moment it was uproar, then Pelham slammed his hand against the wall.

'Quiet!' he shouted. Instantly there was silence. The Doctor had to admit that he was impressed.

Pelham glared at his staff. 'I am going to my office. I want a full report on my desk within ten minutes. Everything else can wait. The most important thing right now is to see whether we have lost any of the fuel barrels.'

The Doctor's respect for the man quickly faded. 'Excuse me...' he butted in. 'I think that the most important thing is, in fact, seeing to the crewman who's been injured. Don't you agree?'

For a moment Pelham looked as though he was going to explode, then he took a deep breath and nodded. 'You are quite right, Doctor. My assistant will show you to the sickbay at once.'

With that, Pelham turned and vanished down the corridor. His assistants followed him meekly.

Matt turned to the Doctor, amazed. 'I've never seen him admit that he's wrong before.'

The Doctor smiled grimly. 'Let's just hope it's the only thing he's wrong about, shall we? Now, where's the sickbay?'

Lizzie was surprised by how small and basic the medical facility was. There were just two beds, surrounded by compact equipment and a small office in one corner. It looked as though the sickbay had been set up to deal with nothing more than minor injuries.

The wounds of the injured man, Bob Clamp, looked far from minor. It looked like some wild beast had clawed him. Lizzie felt sick.

The Doctor's help was gratefully received.

15

The base medic, Beryl, had been able to treat the man's physical injuries fairly easily, but something else was worrying her.

Bob seemed to have a fever. He shifted restlessly in the bed, sweat soaking the sheets and pillows. He kept muttering under his breath. The Doctor leaned close to hear what he had to say.

'He's been like this since he came around,' said Beryl. 'Just keeps saying the same thing over and over.'

'What *is* he saying?' asked Lizzie.

'Nothing that makes sense.' Beryl shook her head. 'The shock must have affected him.'

'Oh, he's making perfect sense.' The Doctor's eyes shone with excitement. 'He's telling us what attacked him. He says that it was a dinosaur!'

Chapter Three

The Doctor ignored the warning about the coming storm. He insisted on going out to look at the site where Bob had been attacked. Despite the cold, Lizzie offered to join him. A grumpy Matt was told to keep an eye on them both.

'What is he doing?' shouted Matt above the howling wind as he watched the Doctor.

'I have no idea,' said Lizzie.

The Doctor was poking around the barrels with what looked like a slim metal torch. The green light from its tip flickered across the snow. There was a high-pitched whine as he swept it back and forth. Snapping the light off, the Doctor peered at a tiny reading on the side of the tube. He was still dressed in nothing warmer than his tweed jacket. Lizzie couldn't work out how he wasn't freezing to death. Even in her windproof anorak and fleece, Lizzie's teeth were chattering so hard that she could barely talk.

'Have you found anything yet?' she called.

'Hmm?' the Doctor looked over at her, brushing snow from his floppy fringe of hair. 'Oh, yes, come and see!'

Lizzie and Matt hurried over to where the Doctor was crouched between the barrels. He had brushed away the loose snow to reveal a deep mark in the frozen ice beneath.

'What does that look like to you?' he asked.

It took Lizzie a few moments to make sense of the shape. Her eyes widened.

Matt realised what it was at about the same time. 'You have got to be kidding...'

'It's a footprint!' gasped Lizzie. 'A huge footprint!'

'Which does tend to back up Mr Clamp's claim that he was attacked by some kind of dinosaur.' The Doctor rose to his feet, peering at the line of footprints leading off into the worsening storm. 'The question is, where did it come from, and where is it now?'

'I've got to tell Mr Pelham,' said Matt nervously.

'And I've got to get some pictures!' Lizzie fumbled under her parka, trying to extract her camera.

'No!' Matt snatched the camera from her. 'There is to be nothing on the record about this until Mr Pelham decides otherwise.'

With that, he turned and started to hurry back towards the base.

'Now you just wait a minute...' Lizzie hurried after him.

The Doctor tried to ignore them. Humans. They were always arguing about the least important things. He chewed his lip. They were in the middle of one of the most remote places on Earth. There was a storm bearing down on them. There was a monster on the loose.

He grinned. 'Someone must have known I was coming!'

With one last glance at the dark sky, the Doctor hurried towards the base. Somehow he had to persuade Pelham to stop work, whilst he worked out exactly what had been disturbed.

'A dinosaur? Rubbish!' Pelham snorted in disbelief. 'This is just another attempt to stop me. You're as bad as those green activists from Wholeweal. Worried about the penguins or the polar bears.'

'Ah, now, not polar bears,' the Doctor started to correct him. 'You only find them at the *North* Pole, not the South. Penguins on the other hand...'

As the two men argued, Lizzie started to edge her way back to the door. She checked to see that Matt wasn't watching her. He was too busy trying to keep his employer calm.

Slipping out into the corridor, she started to make her way back towards the small office where Matt had put her gear. The base was quiet and gloomy. Most of the staff were in the canteen, waiting to see how bad the storm got. She smiled to herself. Her trick with the camera out on the ice had worked perfectly. Now, if anyone noticed that she was missing, they would assume that she had gone back outside to photograph the footprint.

She found Matt's office easily. He had a big plaque on the door that said 'Mr Pelham's Personal Assistant'. She gave a snorting laugh. What an idiot. He hadn't even bothered locking the door. Her black briefcase and camera were sitting on the desk. She closed the door, and then unlocked the clasps on the case with a small key. She checked the equipment inside. Happy that everything was untouched, she closed the case again.

For a moment she hesitated. If she went through with what she had planned then she was finished. No career, no future. Finished. Was what she was doing right?

Then the newspaper on the desk caught her eye. The picture of Rick Pelham's grinning face leered out at her. She had grown up watching men like him destroy the planet. That was why she had joined the Wholeweal protest group in the first place. It was time to fight back.

With new certainty, Lizzie lifted the case down off the desk. With luck, she would be able to find what she was looking for and get back before anyone even noticed that she was missing. She snatched up the camera and slung it over her shoulder. She had to keep up the act of being a determined photographer at all costs.

Lizzie snuck out of the office and into the corridor, peering at the signs and posters that lined the walls. Which way to go? Every part of the base looked the same to her. She set off down a corridor at random, but just found herself in an empty room. The second corridor she tried seemed to end at a blank wall – it must be a part of the base still not finished. Frustrated, Lizzie retraced her steps and tried another direction.

There was a sudden violent gust of wind, enough to rattle the walls of the base. The lights flickered and died. For a moment there was total blackness, then, with the hum of back-up motors, dim, red emergency lights slowly came on.

'Great,' muttered Lizzie. 'Even the man who thinks that he has the solution to the global energy crisis has a power cut.'

She fumbled in her pocket and pulled out a small key ring with a torch on it. Praying that the batteries were still working, she flicked the switch. To her relief, the little light was bright and steady.

She started to edge slowly along the corridor, feeling her way in the gloom. The bland refinery corridors now seemed sinister and dangerous in the eerie red light. The entire complex was bigger than she had thought, and Lizzie started to regret her decision to set off without finding out a bit more about the layout.

She was suddenly aware of movement behind her. She turned just in time to see a dark shadow flash past the end of the corridor. Her heart leapt. If she had been spotted, she would have to bluff it out.

'Hello?' she called out nervously. 'Who's there?'

She peered along the corridor where the figure had gone. Nothing.

Realising that she would soon be missed, she set off in the other direction. Before long, she came to a large door blocking her way. She shone her torch at a sign that read:

DANGER!
POWER ROOM
AUTHORISED PERSONNEL ONLY

She grinned. 'Bingo.'

Setting down the briefcase, she pulled a scrap of paper from her pocket and tapped the numbers written there into the keypad. The heavy door swung open. She gave a sigh of relief. It had taken the promise of a lot of money to persuade Bob Clamp to text the security code to Wholeweal. Lizzie felt a pang of guilt as she recalled how badly injured he was. She hoped he would survive to spend that money.

Checking that she was alone, she slipped inside the power room. It was dark, lit with the same eerie red emergency lights as the rest of the base. Machines lined the walls and in the centre of the floor sat the squat, ugly shape of the power cell. Lizzie hurried over to it, sliding the briefcase under the main body of the machine.

With a pounding heart, she pulled a small plastic box from her pocket. It was about the size and shape of a small mobile phone. She pressed a button on the side. There was a muffled beep from the briefcase.

Stuffing the device back into her pocket, Lizzie hurried back out of the power room.

As she watched the heavy door close, Lizzie let out all her breath in a rush. It was done. For better or worse. Now she had to get back. She turned to retrace her steps.

Something dark rushed at her from the shadows. Lizzie got a sudden glimpse of jet-black eyes and matted fur, and then everything went dark.

Chapter Four

'Lizzie, are you OK?'

Lizzie groaned and forced her eyelids open. She stared groggily up at the figure kneeling over her.

'Doctor?'

'Steady now...' The Doctor helped her to sit against the wall. 'What happened?'

Lizzie rubbed at her scalp. 'I got lost when the lights went out. I was trying to find my way back when—' Her eyes suddenly widened and she clutched at the Doctor's arm. 'It was here! Right here!'

'It's OK.' The Doctor calmed her. 'What did you see?'

Lizzie shook her head. 'I didn't get a proper look. It was dark. I felt fur!'

'Fur?' The Doctor looked puzzled.

'Doctor, this thing wasn't big, not big enough to make those footprints, this was small, like a child...'

The Doctor rubbed his chin thoughtfully. Slowly he reached out and placed his palm on the door of the power room. 'Warm...' he muttered to himself.

There was a sudden whirr of power. The red emergency lights faded as the main lighting came back on. At the same time, there was the sound of footsteps in the corridor and the bellow of a familiar voice.

'I should have guessed that you would be the cause of this!' Pelham snarled at Lizzie. 'Messing about with the power cell, were you?'

The Doctor sprang to his feet, trying his best to calm the situation.

'Now, Mr Pelham. Don't be hasty. She's had a nasty knock on the head.'

'That's nothing to what will happen if she's damaged anything! I knew there was something fishy about you two. From Wholeweal, are you? Here to shut me down?'

'Will you stop being so... suspicious!' cried the Doctor. 'She wasn't interfering with anything! She's a photographer. There's a dinosaur on the loose! What do you think she was trying to do?'

Pelham glared at him, then glanced at the expensive camera slung over Lizzie's shoulder.

'Lizzie says that she was attacked,' said the Doctor calmly. 'The thing that attacked her is probably still inside the base. If we mount a search right away...'

'Thing?' Pelham growled. 'Another dinosaur, I suppose?'

'No, no, no.' The Doctor shook his head. 'This one seemed...' He shot a glance at Lizzie. 'Furry.'

'If there is something on this base then my men will deal with it.' Pelham turned to the guards standing at his shoulder. 'I think that visiting time is over. Get them out of here. Send them back to the ship.'

'That's not going to be possible *just* yet,' said Matt nervously. 'We can't get the helicopter airborne until the storm is over. That could be several hours according to weather control.'

'Then lock them up somewhere!' shouted Pelham. 'Just keep them out of my way. I've got a meeting with the scientific team and I don't want to be disturbed!'

With that, Pelham spun on his heel and swept back down the corridor.

Matt glared at the Doctor and Lizzie in irritation. He held out his hand.

'Your scanning device please, Doctor. Just as a precaution.'

The Doctor reluctantly handed over his sonic screwdriver.

Matt slipped it into his pocket then turned

to the guard captain. 'Lock them up in the storeroom.'

Pelham stamped towards the meeting room in a foul mood. That annoying Doctor had made him look foolish again and he wasn't used to being made to look foolish. On top of everything else, the power cell was obviously faulty. That had been the third power failure in as many days.

He stopped outside the door of the meeting room. Standing in the quiet of the corridor for a moment, he controlled his temper. All that he had to do was wait a few more hours. As soon as the storm died down, they would be able to start loading the first shipment of Fire Ice. Once that was done...

Pelham gave a deep, contented sigh. He was going to be the richest, most powerful man on the planet.

'I just need to remind my... partners, that they must continue with their side of the bargain,' he murmured to himself.

Straightening his tie and smoothing out the creases in his jacket, he unlocked the double doors, and pushed them open.

'Gentlemen,' he said. 'I'm so sorry to have kept you waiting...'

*

'Well at least they're not going to let us starve,' said Lizzie, pulling a biscuit from the packet on the table.

'But they're not Jammie Dodgers, are they?' The Doctor peered at his biscuit in distaste. 'If they'd locked us in here with a packet of Jammie Dodgers, I might have believed Pelham was one of the good guys. But Rich Tea...'

He put the biscuit back on the table and crossed to the door. 'Time for us to get out of here, I think.'

'Seriously?' Lizzie raised an eyebrow at him. 'Are you going to get us into more trouble than we're already in?'

'Absolutely!' The Doctor beamed at her. 'There's a meeting of the scientific team. Lots of scientists. Talking about science stuff. That sounds interesting. I think we ought to be there too, don't you?'

'I've always been keen on science!' Lizzie hurried to his side. 'But we do have the problem of a locked door to deal with. Probably with an armed guard outside.'

'No problem.' The Doctor pulled the torch thing from his pocket. 'Sonic screwdriver.'

Lizzie stared at him in amazement. 'I thought Matt took that off you!'

'He did, but I picked his pocket when he was talking to the guards. Swapped it for a stick of rock with "Southend-on-Sea" right through the middle. It'll be all fluffy by now. Yuck.'

'OK, that takes care of the door. What about the guard?'

The Doctor glanced at his watch. 'Phil? Oh, he should be going about now. Overheard him moaning about missing the football. The rest of the base is probably shutting down because of the storm. Pelham is in his meeting. Matt is doing whatever it is that personal assistants do. Phil checked the lock himself so he knows that we can't possibly get out. Now he thinks he's safe nipping off for ten minutes to check the scores, so...'

The Doctor pressed the tip of his sonic screwdriver to the lock. There was a whine and a flare of green light and the door swung open.

Grabbing Lizzie by the hand, the Doctor crept out into the dark empty corridor.

Finding where Pelham was holding his meeting wasn't that difficult. They just followed the shouting. Pelham's voice rang down the empty corridors.

The Doctor guessed that most of the staff were just trying to keep out of his way.

Pressing an ear to the door of the meeting room, the Doctor tried to listen to what was being said. Pelham's voice was easy enough to make out, but there was something strange about the voices of the other people in the room. Something that seemed familiar to him.

'You told me that we would have no problem extracting the Fire Ice in quantity!' screamed Pelham. 'We had an agreement. If I find that you have gone back on that agreement then you know what will happen! Think about that!'

The Doctor pushed Lizzie back against the wall as Pelham came crashing out of the room, slamming the doors behind him. The Doctor held his breath. If Pelham stopped... If he turned around...

Fortunately Pelham was in too mad a mood. He simply stormed off down the corridor, bellowing for Matt.

'Time for a bit of peace-making, I think,' said the Doctor pulling out his sonic screwdriver.

Unlocking the door, the Doctor barged inside. 'Sorry to interrupt, but I couldn't help overhearing, and it sounds to me as though you could use a good trade union...'

The Doctor tailed off, staring in disbelief at the assembled scientists. From behind him, Lizzie gave a little gasp.

Bright intelligent eyes stared from delicately scaled faces. Elegant crests and fins jutted from the hairless heads. The scientists weren't human.

'What are they?' asked Lizzie in amazement.

The Doctor couldn't keep the surprise from his voice. 'They're Silurians!'

Chapter Five

'You say "Silurians" like I should know what you mean,' said Lizzie, gripping the Doctor's arm nervously. 'Are they aliens?'

'Far from it,' explained the Doctor calmly. 'They are the original rulers of this planet. They were here long before man evolved. Survivors of the race have slept under the ground for millions of years. It seems Mr Pelham has woken them up.'

'Underground lizard men from the dawn of time.' Lizzie nodded. 'Right.'

'Would you close the door, Doctor?' said one of the Silurians calmly. 'We do tend to find the base outside this room rather too cool for comfort.'

'Of course.' The Doctor closed the door and locked it. 'How do you know who I am?'

The Silurian scientist held up a phone. 'The internet is a wonderful source of information, Doctor. It was the work of moments for us to break into the secure files at UNIT. You have been busy in the affairs of this planet.'

'Prehistoric lizard men with smartphones.' Lizzie slumped into a chair. 'It's all a bit much to take in.'

'I am Oclar,' said the Silurian. 'My colleagues are Vondar, Kastac and Eliya.'

'So, this Fire Ice... This wonder fuel that Pelham says he's found. It's not his discovery, is it? It's yours.'

Oclar nodded.

'I knew he couldn't have done it by himself!' said the Doctor happily. 'Didn't I say that he couldn't be cleverer than me?'

'Believe me, Doctor, we do not help him out of choice.'

'Oh?' The Doctor's smile faded.

'Pelham has hostages.'

The Doctor pulled out a chair from the table and sat down. He fixed Oclar with a steady gaze. 'I think that you'd better start at the beginning, don't you?'

The Silurian nodded and sat opposite him.

'We were part of a small scientific task force. When our people were preparing to hibernate – before the arrival of the body that you call the Moon – we were given the task of stockpiling a new fuel source for our eventual revival.'

'The Fire Ice.'

'That is what Pelham calls it, yes. It was a way of preserving fuel for the future. It provides instant clean energy. Pelham found us about a year ago. He was working on a survey of the ice sheet and his instruments picked up our distress beacon.'

'Distress?' asked the Doctor curiously.

'Our base is on the bottom of the underground sea below us. When we retreated to our shelter, this land was warm and green,' explained Oclar. 'To wake and find a world of ice and wind...'

'Not the best situation for a cold-blooded species, I'll admit,' murmured the Doctor.

'We tried to contact others of our race, but could find nothing. Then one day, we had an answer to our distress call.'

'Pelham.'

'Yes. We welcomed any contact with the outside world. He promised that he could act on our behalf, that he could introduce us to the human leaders. But he had one condition...'

'That you provided him with the means of releasing the energy that you had stored.'

'And you believed him?' Lizzie asked in disbelief. 'Someone should have warned you!'

Oclar gave an almost human shrug. 'It

seemed such a perfect solution. You humans are far better at operating at low temperatures than we are. The Fire Ice would be our peace offering, our gift to the human race.'

'So what happened?' asked the Doctor.

'He built a lift shaft to our base – pretending to the world that he was constructing his drilling rig. He and his guards took over our facility one evening. We had not been expecting such treason, and there were too few of us to put up any kind of struggle. He put guards on the hibernation unit with orders to destroy the controls if we resisted. Those of us who were already revived were threatened with being left out on the ice sheet...' Oclar looked away. 'After the first death there was no desire to resist.'

'I'm sorry.' The Doctor kept his voice gentle. 'It was someone close?'

Oclar nodded. 'My daughter.'

The Doctor shot a look at Lizzie, remembering the thing that had surprised her in the corridor. Something small.

'Is there a chance that any of your people have managed to avoid being captured?' he asked. 'A resistance group of some kind?'

'No.' Oclar looked at the Doctor puzzled. 'Why do you ask such a thing?'

'Because someone seems very keen on messing things up for Mr Pelham. Someone with the means to control something large, reptilian and prehistoric...'

The Doctor sprang to his feet and started to pace around the meeting room. 'Now, I know from experience that your hibernation chambers tend to have lots of big, toothy beasts in deep freeze. And I also know that your people have the means of controlling them, directing them. Well, someone seems to be doing just that.'

The Silurian scientists glanced nervously at one another.

'What is it?' asked the Doctor. 'What are you not telling me?'

Oclar said nothing.

'I can help you!' said the Doctor urgently. 'But I need to know everything.'

'The complex beneath us...' said Oclar warily. 'It was not just a scientific research facility. It was also used by our military. A squad of shock troops was frozen, along with several genetically altered specimens.'

'Myrkas.' The Doctor shook his head in despair.

'You know of the Myrkas?' said Oclar in surprise.

'Oh yes.' The Doctor smiled grimly. 'We're old friends.'

'Would one of you mind telling me exactly what a Myrka is?' asked Lizzie, frustrated at being left out.

'A prehistoric creature,' explained the Doctor. 'But one that has been altered to turn it into a creature of war. Able to carry out basic tasks, but basically just a savage killer.'

'That sounds like an unexpected but most welcome bonus!' The rich tones of Rick Pelham boomed from the corridor.

The Doctor and Lizzie spun around to find him standing in the doorway. Behind him were half a dozen armed guards, their guns at the ready.

'So, it would seem that this mysterious "dinosaur" exists after all.' Pelham strode into the room, wagging a finger at the Silurians. 'You've been keeping secrets from me, Oclar. Naughty boy. I thought that I was just going to be able to make money out of the fuel crisis, but it seems that these... Myrkas could have some possibilities in the arms trade too.'

'Listen to me, Pelham,' urged the Doctor. 'You're out of your depth. These creatures are unlike anything you will have seen. Savage, brutal.'

'They sound perfect.' Pelham laughed unpleasantly.

'No.' Lizzie's voice shook with emotion. 'It's gone far enough.'

The Doctor and Pelham turned and looked at her in surprise. She was holding a small black device, like a pager. Her finger poised over a red button on its side.

'Lizzie?' the Doctor frowned at her. 'What's going on? What are you doing?'

'I'm sorry, Doctor.' Her voice was trembling. 'This man, this... monster has to be stopped. There's a bomb in the power room. This is the trigger. I'm going to blow this facility to pieces!'

Chapter Six

'Oh well done, Doctor!' snarled Pelham. 'Just a photographer! Just a journalist after a story! I thought that you were meant to be the clever one. I *knew* that she was from Wholeweal!'

The Doctor did his best to ignore him. He kept his eyes on Lizzie's, aware of her finger on the button of the trigger device. He was also aware that the armed guards now had their weapons aimed at her.

'Lizzie.' He kept his voice calm. 'This isn't you. This isn't the solution.'

'Yes it is,' said Lizzie shakily. 'If Pelham gets his way then the Antarctic will be covered in his factories. Another wilderness lost. Another bit of the planet torn apart just to make him rich.'

'But a bomb? Is that really the way to stop him?'

'This base has a new power-cell system. It's not nuclear, there won't be any fallout, but the bomb will start a chain reaction. There'll be nothing left.'

'And what about the people, Lizzie?' asked the Doctor sadly. 'There are innocent people here. Think of Bob in the sickbay, think about Phil watching the football results, the guards, the caterers. Look around the room. A new species that you've only just met. Scientists from another culture, another time. They can teach you so much. These are the people that you will destroy, not just Pelham.'

He took a step towards her, watching the doubt flicker across her face. 'I know that you feel so helpless. I know that you watch the people around you destroying their world without any thought for the future. I know that you have convinced yourself that this is the only way that you can stand up to them, but you're wrong. This won't make you the winner. This makes you another piece of the problem.'

He held out his hand. 'I've been in your shoes, Lizzie. I've destroyed whole worlds and have had to live with the burden. Believe me, you don't want to press that button.'

There was total silence in the meeting room, every eye on the Doctor and Lizzie. Slowly she bowed her head, and placed the trigger device in the Doctor's hand.

'I'm sorry,' she said quietly.

'I know.' The Doctor let out a long breath. Turning off the trigger device he slipped it into his jacket pocket.

Pelham's guards rushed forward, grabbing Lizzie roughly by the arms.

'Ow!' She struggled in vain. The guards clearly weren't going to take any more chances.

'I'm impressed, Doctor,' said Pelham, eyeing the Doctor with a new respect. 'Perhaps there is more to you than meets the eye after all,'

'There's no need to treat her like that,' snapped the Doctor. 'She won't give you any more trouble.'

'I intend to make sure of that,' said Pelham. 'Take her away and lock her up, and this time do it properly!'

The guards bundled Lizzie roughly out of the room.

'Now, Doctor, give me that trigger device. Then perhaps you can explain to me exactly what these Myrkas are like.'

As the words left Pelham's lips, there was a shattering roar. One wall of the meeting room was ripped to shreds by powerful claws. A huge shape smashed in through the hole, its tough, leathery hide glistening with snowflakes.

'They're like that,' said the Doctor.

Humans and Silurians scattered as the

Myrka tore its way into the base. The guards opened fire in panic. The Doctor dived for cover as bullets whined around the room. Oclar was staring in disbelief at the creature. The Doctor dragged him against the wall as the Myrka lumbered past them. It roared in pain as bullets bounced off it, then it slashed out at the guards with its claws.

It was a far bigger specimen than the last one that the Doctor had seen. It was nearly two and a half metres tall at the shoulder, its four stocky legs rippling with muscle. Two powerful arms jutted from its torso. The claws were razor sharp. The Doctor flinched as the thick, spine-tipped tail thrashed wildly.

'Don't touch its skin!' he shouted. 'It carries a lethal electrical charge!'

The warning came too late for one of the guards. Having run out of bullets, he tried to use his rifle as a club. As the weapon connected with the Myrka's scaly skin, there was a flare of blazing blue light, and the harsh smell of ozone. The man dropped to the floor, dead.

As the Myrka forced its way further into the base a small, fur-covered figure suddenly appeared through the ragged hole torn in the wall.

'Father!'

Oclar stared in amazement. 'Partock?'

The figure pulled back a heavy fur hood to reveal the delicately scaled face of a young Silurian girl. Oclar embraced her warmly. 'I thought that you were dead!'

'I've no time to explain now!' said the girl, shaking herself free from him. 'We must go whilst we have the chance.'

Oclar stared fearfully at the driving snowstorm outside. Already the temperature in the base had dropped alarmingly. 'We won't last long out there...'

'Oh, I'm guessing Partock has thought of that already, hmm?' asked the Doctor.

Partock shot him a wary glance.

'Who is this? Another of Pelham's thugs?'

'No.' Oclar shook his head. 'He's a friend.'

For a moment, the young Silurian looked as though she was going to argue, then she gave a brisk nod. 'Good. I'll need your help to get Father and the others to the lift building.'

'What about your pet?' The Doctor jerked a thumb at the rampaging Myrka. 'You can call it off now.'

'Let it finish what it's started,' snarled Partock. 'The humans deserve no better.'

'I can't let you do that.' The Doctor's voice was stern. 'It's served its purpose as a diversion.

Now call it off.'

'No.' Partock glared at him.

The Doctor held her gaze. 'You won't be able to get all your people out of here without my help, and the longer we stand here in the cold the weaker they are going to get.'

Time Lord and Silurian stared at each other for what seemed like an age, then Partock reached into her furs and pulled out a small flute-like device. She raised it to her lips and blew. An electronic warbling filled the air and the Myrka's head twitched upright. It was almost like a dog responding to its master's whistle

'It will return to its lair,' said Partock grumpily.

'What a well-behaved little Myrka it is.' The Doctor beamed at her.

Partock pulled the furs tightly around her head and grasped her father's arm. The scientists were already shivering violently. She started to guide everyone out through the ragged hole in the base wall.

The Doctor hesitated for a moment, torn between getting the scientists to safety and going back in to rescue Lizzie. With a shake of his head he realised that if he was to mount any kind of any rescue attempt then he needed

Oclar and Partock's help.

Reluctantly, he turned and followed the small party of Silurians through the gap in the wall.

Chapter Seven

As they stepped out into the wind, one of the Silurian scientists cried out in pain and stumbled. The Doctor dragged him back to his feet.

It was bitter, and the storm was whipping the snow into swirling, biting clouds. The tall spire of the drill-head building was a faint shape through the blizzard. It was probably no more than a few hundred metres away, but the cold-blooded Silurians were already starting to struggle in the severe conditions.

Partock half-dragged, half-carried her father forward. The Doctor urged the others on. From behind them, there was the grinding of metal and plastic as the Myrka tore itself free from the base. With a final shattering roar, it vanished into the storm. Soon there was only the sound of blaring alarms and terrified voices.

The Doctor just hoped that Lizzie had been taken somewhere well out of harm's way. Her actions had made him angry and sad at the same time. Angry that he had been so sure she was who she claimed, and sad that she had felt that she had to go down such an extreme path. He had seen in her eyes how torn she had been. Would she really have blown them all sky high? In his hearts, he didn't think so. He hoped that he would get a chance to ask her.

As they arrived at the drill-head building, the scientists were shaking with cold. One of them, the eldest, was almost in a coma. Even Partock in her heavy furs was starting to get slow and sluggish. She fumbled with the locked door, her fingers numb with cold.

'Here, let me help.' The Doctor drew her gently to one side, slipping the sonic screwdriver from his jacket pocket.

He pressed the nozzle of the screwdriver to the door. A familiar whine and blaze of green light filled the air. The door opened and a blast of warmth wafted out. The Doctor and Partock dragged the Silurians inside the building.

The Doctor closed the door and hurried over to a heating control on the wall. He twisted it to full. There was the whine of distant motors, and warm air started to flood into the room.

Oclar gave a hiss of pleasure as his body temperature started to rise once more. 'Thank you, Doctor. We would not have survived much longer.'

'No, the Antarctic really isn't a good place for Silurians to be.' He glanced over at Partock. 'You've been lucky to survive.'

'Lucky?' Partock scoffed. 'There has been nothing lucky about it.'

'What happened?' asked the Doctor gently. 'What happened after Pelham left you out on the ice?'

Partock was silent for a moment, then took a deep breath.

'I lay in the snow, watching as Pelham took my father and the others back to the base. He assumed that the cold would kill me, and it nearly did. I almost died right there, but then I looked at what you apes have done to my world. A world made cold and damp and dark. In the end it was hatred that kept me alive. Hatred of humanity.'

The room had gone quiet, everyone listening to Partock's story.

'I forced myself to stand, to follow the tracks left by Pelham's machines. At last I stumbled across a series of primitive wooden structures, nothing more than shacks.'

'An abandoned whaling station,' murmured the Doctor to himself. Partock ignored him.

'Inside were clothes, stinking rotten furs that kept out the cold. I found crude bladed weapons and hunted the mammals that swim beneath the ice. I forced myself to eat their flesh. Slowly, I regained my strength.'

Oclar reached out to lay a hand on his daughters shoulder, but Partock brushed it aside.

'Wrapping myself in the furs I made it back to the base. I needed somewhere warm to hide where I could plan my revenge.'

'The power room,' said the Doctor.

Partock nodded. 'Pelham's guards are even more stupid than the rest of the apes. Hiding from them was easy. I learned how to tamper with the controls. I could plunge the base into darkness whenever I wished. The humans do not deal well with the dark. Perhaps a part of them remembers how we used to hunt them in the forests of the old world. It was easy for me to use the shadows to find what I needed, to make my way back down to our base beneath the ice.'

Oclar shook his head. 'But how did you find out about the Myrka herds, the military? Those files were secret, known only to me and a handful of others.'

'You are too trusting, Father. It was easy to

break into your secret files and learn the true nature of our facility. I revived the Myrkas to attack the humans!'

'You have gone too far, daughter!' Oclar voice was shaking with anger. 'You will only make the situation with the humans worse!'

'The Myrkas will provide the means to bring the humans to their knees! We can wipe out the rest of these primitives with ease!'

'No! I will not allow it!'

The Doctor hurried over to the lift. 'I think we should get down there, pronto. We don't want a herd of grumpy Myrkas stamping about the place. If they've been unfrozen, it should be easy enough to refreeze them.'

The lift door slid open and the Doctor stepped back in shock.

Standing in the doorway was a giant figure, its sleek form clad in combat gear. Black eyes glinted wickedly from beneath a fierce-looking helmet as the figure raised a disk-like gun.

It was a Sea Devil.

Chapter Eight

'Die, human.' The creature's hissing voice was filled with hatred.

'No!' Partock knocked the weapon aside. 'This human is helping us.'

The Sea Devil hissed angrily, but lowered its weapon. From the shadows emerged other Sea Devils, all heavily armed. The Doctor chewed his lip nervously. Their body armour marked them out as a commando squad of highly trained killers. It didn't bode well.

'Is everything ready?' asked Partock.

'We await your command.'

'What is the meaning of this?' Oclar pushed forward, struggling to speak through chattering teeth. 'You had no right to revive the military...'

'I had no choice,' snapped Partock. 'Pelham and the rest of the apes cannot be trusted. They need force to control them. General Veldac's troops will provide that force.'

'Um, excuse me.' The Doctor waved a nervous hand in the air. 'I don't mean to put a spanner in what I assume is a carefully worked out plan, but Pelham did mention that he had guards in the hibernation chambers.'

'And you thought that I hadn't already dealt with them?' Partock shot a despairing look at him, and then turned to the Sea Devil commander. 'Start your attack.'

Pelham slumped behind his desk, mopping at his forehead with a tissue.

'Where is it?' he asked one of the guards. 'Is it following us?'

'No, sir.' The guard listened intently to the voice in his earpiece. 'My men followed the creature for about half a mile. It appears to have gone into a fracture in the ice sheet.'

'Then it came from the underground lake,' mused Pelham.

'PelCorp is committed to having a minimal impact on the environment.' Lizzie was reading from a poster on his wall. 'I'm not sure you're going to be able to claim that you've met that particular target, are you?'

'Shut up and sit down,' Pelham snarled at her. 'I have had just about enough of people like you. I should have spotted you from the very beginning. Eco-warriors.' He spat the word.

'But your little game is up, isn't it, Pelham?' taunted Lizzie. 'You might have pulled the wool over people's eyes with promises of wealth from your miraculous new fuel, but you're not going to be able to hide an entire new species. Prehistoric creatures. It's over for you!'

'You think so?' Pelham raised an eyebrow at her. 'My company and my staff have been attacked by a hostile force. People have been killed, and property has been destroyed. I believe that means I have a right to defend myself.'

Lizzie's eyes widened. 'You're going to destroy the hibernation equipment, aren't you? You're going to wipe out an entire race!'

'It's a bit late for you to worry about destroying innocents.' Pelham gave a short barking laugh and snapped on the intercom on his desk. 'Get me the guard captain at the drill head.'

'I was about to inform you, sir.' The voice was tinny over the speaker. 'We've lost all contact with the drill head. That creature has probably destroyed some cables. It could take some time to repair the damage.'

Pelham sat back in his chair, lips pursed. 'The creature, or something else?'

'Then there's nothing you can do but wait,' said Lizzie.

'I think we can do better than that. The Navy have been very interested in this operation. After all, the fuel is of huge benefit to them as well. I'm sure that they will be only too keen to help me deal with "foreign agents".' He picked up a phone on his desk. 'Get me Admiral Turner.'

In the control room far below the ice sheet, all was a picture of quiet calm. Silurian scientists hurried back and forth between banks of equipment. Pumps and filters hummed with power as the Fire Ice was collected and refined. The only things that spoilt the illusion of a happy, well-run facility were the guns in the hands of the human guards stationed around the walls.

One of the guards looked up idly as the glowing numbers above the lift door started to count steadily downwards. Frowning, he glanced down at his watch. There wasn't a shift change due for another hour. The only other person authorised to come down to the lab was Pelham, and if he was going to visit then his fussy assistant normally phoned in advance.

Lifting his rifle, the guard started to make his way across to the lift. Someone was going to get in a lot of trouble if the correct procedure hadn't been followed.

He took a deep breath ready to bawl out whichever poor unfortunate had been sent down. The lift doors slid apart.

The guard barely had a chance to take in what he was seeing before the blast from a Sea Devil gun took him down. The Sea Devils swarmed out of the lift, targeting the guards with ruthless aim. The fight was over in a matter of moments.

The Doctor stepped slowly from the lift and looked around sadly at the human bodies that now littered the control room. They had never stood a chance. All around him the Silurian scientists were greeting each other warmly, glad that their ordeal was over.

Oclar laid a scaly hand on the Doctor's shoulder. 'I'm sorry. These deaths were not my intention.'

'I know.' The Doctor smiled sadly. 'But let's see if we can make them the last, eh?'

Oclar nodded.

'Now that you have captured the base, what are we going to do?' the Doctor asked.

Oclar took a deep breath. 'Speak with the

humans. Only this time, we will do it on our terms, not Pelham's.'

The Sea Devil commander, Veldac, hissed in displeasure. 'Is that wise, Oclar? The apes have already proved that they cannot be trusted. Surely we should keep the fuel source for ourselves.'

'But my original plan is sound. If we come to them offering the fuel as a gift then they must see that our intentions are peaceful.'

'It is still a good plan,' Partock stood alongside her father. 'We shouldn't give up on peaceful solutions, Veldac, just because of one greedy human.'

'I'm delighted to hear that!' said the Doctor in surprise. 'I thought that you were the one I was going to have trouble with!'

'I had to get my father free,' said Partock stubbornly. 'I couldn't have done it without Veldac and his troops.'

'And I am grateful,' said Oclar. 'In the meantime, I need to check that Pelham's haste to extract the Fire Ice has not caused damage to our machinery.'

'I'll help you,' said the Doctor.

As he followed the Silurian scientist to the main control bank, a smile flickered across Partock's face. 'My father is a fool, Veldac. Let him give the Fire Ice to the humans. A fine gift indeed. As soon as they use it, their species is doomed and the planet is ours.'

Chapter Nine

Lizzie peered out of the window of the storeroom where she had been locked up. Pelham's men were starting to load the drums of Fire Ice. Ever since the storm had eased, there had been a steady stream of tractors and snow mobiles. In a matter of hours, Pelham would be showing the first sample of his super fuel to the world, and he would have won.

She thumped the windowsill in frustration. 'Where the hell have you got to, Doctor?' she muttered under her breath.

At first, the Doctor had been nothing more than a way of getting here, a decoy. But now she was beginning to realise just how much she owed him. He had stopped her from making a terrible mistake. The disappointment in his eyes had been more than she could bear. More than anything, she wanted to show him that he had been right about her, and that she would never have pressed that button.

A low, drumming throb filled the air, and Lizzie's heart sank as two huge dark shapes swung low over the base. They were Navy helicopters.

The aircraft settled onto the ground in a blizzard of snow and ice. The doors of the helicopters slid open and dozens of heavily armed troops started to fan out in a well-drilled pattern.

Pelham's back-up had arrived.

There were other eyes watching as the troops arrived, eyes that took everything in with a professional interest.

Noting the number and position of the human troops, the Sea Devil scout slipped through the neat hole that had been cut through the ice. They had cut holes like this all over the ice sheet with their heat weapons. It allowed them to spy on the humans unseen.

Adjusting the heating control on his thermal armour the Sea Devil scout swam through the freezing water with powerful strokes. The Sea Devils were far more suited to water than land. The scout wished that the heavy thermal armour was not necessary. They had far more resistance to cold than their Silurian cousins. Even so, the freezing waters of the Antarctic would quickly prove fatal if not for the heating units the armour contained.

Kicking out with thickly webbed feet, the scout made his way to the airlock deep beneath the ice. Working the controls, he made his way into the base. Veldac was already waiting for him.

'What is your report?' hissed the General.

'The humans have brought in troops, as you suspected, General. A force of about thirty soldiers has arrived in two of their flying machines.'

'The humans are predictable, but their desire to keep the Fire Ice will make them cautious.'

'The force is small, sir, and their weapons are primitive. Shall we destroy them now?'

'Not yet. You will return to your post, and inform me if the humans start any action against us.'

'Yes, General.' The scout saluted sharply, and turned back towards the airlock.

The General turned to his aide. 'Tell Partock that our plan is entering its final stage.'

'Intelligent lizards? Is this some kind of a joke?' The Navy captain stared at Pelham as if he was mad.

Pelham gave him a humourless smile. 'I imagine that information about these creatures is passed down on a need-to-know basis. Am I right, Admiral?'

Admiral Turner nodded. 'The creatures exist, Captain. They are intelligent, aggressive and armed with heat weapons unlike anything that you will have seen before. Your orders are to shoot on sight.'

To his credit, the captain took in this extraordinary information with barely a flicker of surprise. 'Sir.'

'They will almost certainly try and stop us getting the barrels of Fire Ice to the ship,' said Pelham. 'That must not be allowed to happen.'

'And the drill head?'

'Is currently under the control of these creatures. We daren't risk a full assault. They could simply destroy the equipment and the fuel source.'

'Your orders, sir?'

'Evacuate all personnel. Secure the fuel that has already been extracted, then give these lizards a simple choice. Either they surrender or we destroy them.'

The Doctor and Oclar were deep in the bowels of one of the hibernation machines when General Veldac's aide entered the control room.

Partock hurried over to him. 'Well?'

'The humans have called in troops.'

Partock nodded. 'We suspected this would happen. Does the General understand what he has to do?'

'Yes, Partock.'

'Good.'

The Doctor hurried over. 'I do hope that we're not going to do anything hasty. Troops tend to have guns and twitchy trigger fingers. We really don't want to do anything that would upset them.'

'Upset them, Doctor? Far from it.'

'They are almost certainly going to try and get the first treatment of Fire Ice away from here. We need to stop them doing that if we are going to have any chance of doing a deal with them. Now, my plan is this—'

'We're not going to stop them, Doctor,' said Partock. 'We're going to let them take it.'

'Let them?'

'But of course. The General will make it look very convincing, but the humans will escape with their precious fuel.'

'I don't understand, daughter...' Oclar looked confused.

'What have you done?' The Doctor's voice was suddenly steely. Partock stared at him

67

in defiance. The Doctor gripped her by the arms. 'When the security guard caught you sneaking around by the barrels, you weren't trying to destroy them, were you? You want them to take the fuel so you must have done something to it. Now tell me what!'

Partock shook herself free. 'I've added an artificial boosting agent to the barrels.'

Oclar went pale. 'Dear Maker...'

'What will it do, Oclar?' asked the Doctor urgently. 'Quickly!'

'It will change the rate at which the fuel is released from the ice. It will speed up the process a thousand times.'

'And what will that mean?'

'Huge quantities of greenhouse gases will be released. It will speed up the warming of this planet. It will do precisely the reverse of what the humans hope this fuel will achieve!'

The Doctor stared at Partock in disbelief. 'You'll set off a chain reaction that will destroy most of the life on this planet. Not just the humans, but plant life, animal life, everything.'

'It will return this planet to a state where we can live properly,' roared Partock. 'When we extract the rest of the fuel and I add the boosting agent, it will return this planet to how it was in our own time. This is the gift that I give to the humans.'

'Partock, please,' begged Oclar. 'Don't do this!'

'You are weak and old, Father,' said Partock with a sneer. 'I knew that you would never agree to this plan. That is why I revived Veldac and his troops. They at least have the courage to do what is needed.'

'No.' The Doctor shook his head. 'It won't work, Partock. This planet isn't the same as it was when you ruled. The environment, the climate, everything has changed. You *can't* turn it back to how it was!' He turned and started towards the lift. 'I've got to get in touch with Pelham. Tell him that he mustn't ship those barrels.'

Partock stepped into his path. 'Foolish ape.'

Her tongue spat from her mouth, whiplashing onto the Doctor's neck.

The effect of the venom was instant. The Doctor crashed to the floor.

Chapter Ten

'Oh, my head.' The Doctor forced his eyelids open to find Oclar looking at him in concern.

'Take it easy, Doctor. You're still very weak,' said the Silurian.

'Very weak? That's the understatement of the year. I haven't felt this bad since I went out on the town with Oscar Wilde.' He shook his head, trying to clear his blurred vision. 'Hang on a mo. I should be dead, shouldn't I? I thought that Silurian venom was deadly.'

'Not the venom of young Silurians,' explained Oclar. 'It takes time for the venom sacs to reach full strength. You were lucky.'

'Really?' said the Doctor groggily. 'So this is what lucky feels like, is it? If this is lucky, then I can do without being lucky ever again.' He gave a deep sigh and glared at Oclar. 'What is it with the youth of today? First Lizzie and now Partock. Is it only the adults who can behave like... well, like adults?' He shook his head. 'How long have I been out?'

Oclar shrugged. 'An hour, maybe more.'

'An hour! I don't have time to be lying around here for an hour!' The Doctor clambered to his feet, swaying unsteadily.

He looked around at the scientists working calmly at the machinery in the control room. 'Where are our Sea Devil friends?'

'General Veldac is leading his troops.' The Doctor turned to find that Partock was watching him with interest. 'You must be stronger than you look, human,' she went on. 'I thought that I had killed you.'

'Well, I'm not human, and you youngsters do tend to overestimate your abilities.'

Partock bristled. 'Careful, Doctor. I have told the General to leave most of the apes alive on the surface. It will make their escape look more convincing. But I can always change those orders.'

'Yes, you probably can,' said the Doctor sadly. 'You don't need to do this, Partock. I can make this right, you know.'

The young Silurian ignored him and unclipped a communicator from her belt. 'General, are you ready to start your attack?'

'Yes, Partock.'

As Partock turned away, the Doctor's eye dropped to the whistle-like device at her belt.

'The Myrka control,' he muttered to himself.

72

Careful to conceal what he was doing, he rummaged in his pocket for his sonic screwdriver. As he did so, his fingers touched something else. It was the trigger device he had taken from Lizzie.

A smile flickered across the Doctor's lips.

'What are you up to, Doctor?' whispered Oclar. 'If my daughter suspects anything...'

The Doctor grinned at him. 'I know how to stop her. You'd better cover your ears, Oclar, it's going to get noisy around here!'

Veldac turned off his communicator and watched as the last of the barrels of Fire Ice was loaded onto one of the human machines. A small convoy of vehicles was now lined up on the ice, ready to make the journey to the coast.

Each vehicle was guarded by two of the human soldiers. Veldac had fought in enough battles to tell that each man was on a knife edge.

He glanced at his own soldiers. They too were alert and ready for his signal. The Sea Devil allowed himself a smile of satisfaction. They had been too long frozen in the ice. It was good to be in battle once more.

He raised the disk of his heat weapon and

took careful aim at the human soldier nearest to him. His task was only to drive the humans away, and make it look as though they had escaped. He had been instructed to keep injuries to a minimum.

He hissed in disgust. There was a time when they hunted the human apes freely. But he was a soldier and this was war. Casualties were inevitable.

He pressed the trigger, sending a blast of super-concentrated heat streaming towards the convoy. There was a brief, intense burst of flame, and a soldier was turned into a pillar of fire.

At once there was mayhem. The human soldiers dived for cover, opening fire with their weapons. Others tried to help their burning colleague. At the same time, Veldac's troops surged from their holes in the ice, falling snow turning to steam as it landed on their heated armour.

The air was filled with the charring smell of the heat guns and the whine of bullets.

Veldac's turtle-like lips pulled back in a contented smile.

'Advance!' he hissed.

Lizzie had watched in horror as the lizard

things started their attack. They emerged from nowhere, taking the Navy completely by surprise. Within moments, though, the troops had taken up defensive positions. Now a vicious battle raged out on the ice.

As they desperately tried to hold the creatures back, she could see the civilian members of the crew making a dash for the convoy of tractors. In the distance she could see technicians preparing Pelham's helicopter to leave.

All this time she had been worried about what Pelham was going to do with her. Suddenly it was obvious. He was just going to leave her behind!

'Hey!' bellowed Lizzie, banging on the glass. 'Wait. I'm still locked up in here! Don't forget about me!'

A searing beam of heat suddenly blasted through the window. Glass flew everywhere and Lizzie was hurled to the ground.

A jagged hole had been blasted in the wall. There was a choking, burning smell as the walls of the storeroom charred and blistered. Icy wind swept through the hole. As she staggered to her feet, Lizzie realised that this was her chance to escape.

She struggled into one of the heavy fur-lined

parkas that hung by the door then scrambled out through the side of the storeroom and into the freezing air.

As she stumbled away from the base, Lizzie realised that she was probably no safer outside. The air was filled with the zing of bullets and the harsh buzz of heat guns. There was the blast of an explosion as one of the soldiers hurled a grenade at the advancing lizard men.

Lizzie waded through thigh-deep snow, desperate to find a place of safety.

As she rounded the corner of the building a tall shadow loomed over her. Lizzie stared up in horror as a Sea Devil raised its heat gun.

Chapter Eleven

'This could be painful, Oclar...' The Doctor looked at the scientist with concern. 'And I can't promise that I'm going to be able to find the right frequency straight away. Are you ready?'

The Silurian nodded, clamping his hands over his ears.

Taking a deep breath the Doctor pointed his sonic screwdriver at the signalling device on Partock's belt and pressed the button.

The noise that filled the undersea base was deafening. The Silurians reeled in pain, clutching at their heads.

Partock turned, hatred in her eyes. 'You again! This time I will kill you.' She reached for her heat gun, and scrabbled to turn off the screaming device at her belt.

'No, no, no!' The Doctor frantically adjusted controls on the screwdriver. 'Come on, come on! That frequency has got to be there somewhere!'

The noise from the signalling device went

up in pitch, almost too high for the Doctor to hear. The effect on Partock and the rest of the Silurians was instant. They collapsed on the spot.

On the surface of the ice, Lizzie closed her eyes, waiting for the blast of heat that would end her life.

It never came.

She opened one eye nervously. The Sea Devil was lying flat on its back in the snow. So were all the others. All around her she could see the naval force slowly advancing on their floored attackers. Lizzie nudged the Sea Devil with her foot. It moved weakly. It wasn't dead, then, just stunned somehow.

She grinned. No prizes for guessing who was responsible. Aware that she probably only had a matter of moments before the Navy moved in to secure their prisoners, she knelt by the prone Sea Devil. She lifted the gun between its webbed fingers, grimacing at the slimy feel of its skin. Attached to the creature's belt was a small black device. A communicator.

'Well, if the Doctor is behind all this...' Lizzie unclipped it and pressed the transmit button. 'Doctor? Are you there?'

*

78

'*Doctor?*'

The Doctor was helping a dazed and dizzy Oclar to his feet when Lizzie's voice rang out through the control room. He snatched up Partock's communicator in delight.

'Lizzie Davies! You beauty! Where are you?'

'*Out on the ice sheet with lots of unconscious sea-lizard thingies. Is that your doing?*'

'They're called Sea Devils,' explained the Doctor. 'Well... They're not *actually* called Sea Devils. That's a less than flattering nickname coined back in the 1970s, but let's call them that for the moment. Are they all out cold? They should all be out cold.'

'*Cold and getting colder by the minute.*'

'And Pelham?'

'*Getting ready to leave with his precious barrels.*'

'Listen, Lizzie,' said the Doctor urgently. 'This is very important. He mustn't leave. I'll explain everything later, but for the moment all you need to know is that the Fire Ice has been sabotaged. If Pelham tries to use that fuel, it will be the end of everything. This is what I want you to do...'

Lizzie listened as the Doctor outlined his plan. As he explained what it was that he wanted her to do, all she wanted to do was to run away in terror. But this was her chance to prove to the Doctor just what she was really made of.

Tucking the Sea Devil communicator into her jacket, she hurried back in through the jagged hole in the refinery wall. The door to the storeroom was still locked. With a shrug, Lizzie raised the Sea Devil gun and fired it at the lock. The door exploded into flaming fragments. Nodding with satisfaction, Lizzie stepped through into the corridor beyond.

The base was in uproar. Between the Myrka attack and the damage caused by the Sea Devil guns, the place was practically falling apart. Technicians and guards rushed past Lizzie, desperate to get to the waiting tractors.

Lizzie turned the other way. She had to find Pelham. He had something she needed. She tucked the gun into her parka and pulled up the hood to disguise her features. Then she set off towards his office.

Far below in the Silurian base, the Doctor made his way from the control room towards the hibernation chamber. He casually tossed the signalling device from hand to hand. He was worried. He had hoped that he would be able to find a better solution than the one he was about to use. Sadly time was against him. The arrival of the Navy troops was hardly unexpected, but it had not helped things. Now it was a race against time.

'Humans,' muttered the Doctor to himself. 'I really don't know why I like them so much.'

Passing through the hibernation control centre, the Doctor made his way to a wide expanse of rock wall. He raised his sonic screwdriver, sending green light dancing across the rock. With a grinding of stone on stone, the entrance to the secret military part of the base slid open.

The Doctor hurried down a wide passage carved from the rock. The passage led to a narrow walkway overlooking a vast underground chamber. He pressed a control on the metal rail and the chamber was flooded with light.

He stood for a moment, marvelling at the ambition of the Silurian race. To work so hard to ensure that they survived, only to find that others had taken advantage of their absence. To find a race in charge that had been nothing but primitive apes when they had started their long sleep. The previous attempts at getting the two species to work together had ended in disaster. It seemed as though this time wasn't going to be any different.

The Doctor stood, staring down at the cavern below him. He was aware that what he was about to do was unlikely to help relations between the two species. Then he pressed the button on the signalling device.

The chamber was suddenly filled with shattering roars as the machinery shut down. Far below him, huge creatures stirred in the slowly swirling vapour. Huge creatures that the Earth had not seen for millions of years. An army of Myrkas was waking!

Chapter Twelve

When the Doctor returned to the hibernation control room, he found that Oclar had dragged all of the stunned Silurians there. Now he was placing them back into their hibernation cocoons.

The Doctor watched as Oclar gently laid his daughter back into her own freezer pod. Oclar's hand hesitated over the controls.

'She isn't really evil, you know, Doctor, just... misguided. Angry about the way that fate has treated our people. Eager to put things right'

'I know,' said the Doctor gently. 'It's a very... human trait.'

Oclar smiled at him, and pressed his hand down on the control panel. A glass screen slid down over Partock's cocoon, and wisps of icy gas started to flood the inside.

'Oclar, what I'm about to do...' The Doctor hesitated. 'There is no way of knowing when your people will revive again.'

'I had guessed as much.' The Silurian gave

a deep sigh. 'The time is not yet right. The humans are not ready for the gift I offered. And we are not ready either. I hope that when I next awake the world will be a different place. And if I don't awake...' He shrugged. 'Then perhaps that is for the best.'

The Doctor held out a steadying arm as the Silurian scientist climbed into his own hibernation cocoon. For a moment, Oclar stared into the Doctor's eyes.

'And what about you, Doctor? How long will you keep trying to teach these humans that you regard so highly?'

The Doctor smiled. 'For as long as it takes.'

The Doctor pressed a button on the console, and the glass screen slid down. As the icy mist flooded the chamber the Doctor turned and walked back to the lift. The doors opened with a soft chime and the Doctor stepped inside. As they closed behind him, he didn't look back.

Lizzie needn't have worried about being seen. Everyone on the base was far too concerned with escaping to worry about a random stranger. Reaching Pelham's office without being stopped was easier than she had thought.

Clutching the Sea Devil gun beneath her jacket, she listened at the door. Pelham's gruff tones were unmistakable, as was Matt's nasal whine. Lizzie took a deep breath, pulled the gun from her jacket, and pushed open the door.

Pelham and Matt were bundling papers and CDs into a number of metal cases. Both men looked up in surprise as she burst into the room. Their expressions were almost comical. There was almost admiration in Pelham's voice as he recovered himself.

'Miss Davies. It appears that we are unable to find a room capable of holding you!' His eyes flashed to the gun in her hand. 'And you seem to have provided me with a superb example of Silurian weaponry. Perhaps I'm wrong in trying to lock you up all the time. I should make you my personal assistant instead!'

Lizzie closed the office door with her foot. She kept the gun pointed at the two men. 'Not sure I like the company I'd be working for.'

She could see her black case with the bomb inside sitting on a table on the far side of the office. Pelham followed her gaze. 'Ah... So that's what you came for. Still trying to save the world?'

Lizzie laughed. 'That's more true than you might think. Your miracle fuel? Your Fire Ice that will solve the energy crisis? The Silurians have tampered with it. They've added something that changes it somehow. If you try to use what's in those barrels then you're going to change the climate for ever.'

'I don't believe you!' snapped Pelham. 'Oclar would never...'

'Not Oclar. His daughter, Partock. And after what you did to her, I can hardly say that I blame her.'

'So she survived. How clever of her.' Pelham's face twisted in anger. 'Damn her. But it's not too late. If we can get a sample of the fuel, we can analyse what she's done.'

'Oh no.' Lizzie covered him with the gun. 'It's over Pelham. Now, pick up the case. We're going back to the power room.'

'Don't be stupid. If we're quick, we can rescue this.'

'It's too late to salvage anything. Now do as I say and pick up the case.'

Pelham hesitated, but it was clear that Lizzie was in no mood to be toyed with. He lifted the case, licking his lips nervously as he eyed the gleaming bomb inside.

'If you explode this thing...'

'I'm not going to explode anything,' said Lizzie innocently. 'The Doctor has the trigger, and he's not going to use it until everyone is safely out of here. The only thing that he intends to destroy is the base, the drill head and the barrels.'

'The Doctor,' growled Pelham. 'I should have known that he'd end up siding with you. You'll never get away with this. Admiral Turner and his men—'

'Are going to have their hands full.'

Pelham frowned at her. 'What do you mean?'

'You'll see.' Lizzie waved the gun at him and Matt. 'Now move.'

The Navy captain was wondering what he was going to do with the bodies of several large, intelligent lizards when the first roar reached him. Screams of panic and the rattle of gunfire followed.

Snatching up his rifle, he raced towards the noise. As he rounded the corner of the base, he stopped and stared in disbelief at the scene in front of him.

A huge, dinosaur-like monster was hauling itself from a ragged hole in the ice. His men were firing madly, trying to hold the creature back, but with no effect.

Taking aim at the beast, the captain fired several shots. The monster turned its massive head and snarled menacingly at him.

PelCorp personnel were scattering in panic. The captain yelled at his second-in-command. 'Sergeant! Get those people to the helicopters!'

As the words left his mouth, there was another monstrous bellow from behind him. He spun to see another creature hauling itself from the ice, and another, and another!

Realising that they were rapidly being outnumbered, the captain gave the only order he could.

'Retreat!'

It didn't take long to reach the power room. The base was almost deserted. Keeping the gun aimed at Pelham and Matt the whole time, Lizzie made them push the case of explosives back underneath the power cell, then guided them back out into the corridor.

'Now, stand back,' said Lizzie.

She raised the Sea Devil gun and aimed it at the lock. There was a buzz of power, and a ray of searing heart melted the lock into molten waste.

Lizzie nodded in satisfaction. 'That's just in case you had any ideas about getting back inside to disarm it.' She fumbled in the pocket of her jacket for the communicator. She had to let the Doctor know that she was ready.

That brief lapse in Lizzie's focus was all Pelham needed. He lashed out at her, jarring her wrist and sending the heat gun flying. Lizzie made a lunge for it, but she was too late. Matt scooped up the gun and levelled it at her menacingly.

Pelham snatched the communicator from her hand. 'You little idiot. Did you really think you'd get away with it?'

'Mr Pelham.' Matt was eyeing the power room door nervously. 'We should get away from here, sir. The bomb...'

Pelham smiled. 'The Doctor's not going to detonate it until he knows his little friend here is safe. So now I've got something to bargain with.' He grabbed Lizzie by the arm. 'You're coming with us. We'll fly back to the container ship and contact the Doctor from there.'

Pelham and Matt set off for the helicopter pad, pushing the protesting Lizzie in front of them. As they stepped out into the freezing air and made their way towards the waiting helicopter, Pelham gave Lizzie an unpleasant smile.

'I really have to thank you, my dear. If what you say about the fuel is true, if it really is contaminated, then I might have come away from this with nothing. But that weapon could be a much more valuable source of income. PelCorp Thermal Weapons. It has a nice ring to it, don't you think?'

Before Lizzie could even think of a witty reply, there was a terrifying roar. The huge shape of a Myrka lumbered through the snow towards them. It bared its teeth in a savage snarl.

As they turned to run, there was another thunderous roar and a second creature emerged from around the corner of the base.

They were cut off.

Chapter Thirteen

Pelham pushed Matt forward, screaming at him in terror. 'Use the gun, man, use the gun!'

Matt raised the heat gun with trembling hands, taking aim at the towering monsters.

'No!' The shout came spiralling through the wind. 'Don't do it!'

The Doctor appeared through the snow, racing towards them. The Myrka nearest to them turned its head towards the noise. Ignoring the Doctor's shouted warning, Matt pressed the trigger.

The beam of heat seared into the Myrka's side filling the air with the reek of charred flesh. It reared up, shrieking in pain. Matt fired again and again. This time, the Myrka turned its huge head, looking for the thing that was hurting it.

Matt stared upwards as the Myrka bore down on him. A huge claw lifted into the air.

And slammed down.

The Myrkas started to turn on the injured one. They began to fight amongst themselves, driven into a feeding frenzy by the smell of blood. The Doctor fumbled in his pocket as one of the creatures started to lurch towards them.

'Don't move!' he hissed.

Lizzie's eyes widened in horror as the Myrka got closer and closer. The Doctor was still mucking about with his sonic screwdriver.

Lizzie closed her eyes. She could almost feel the monster's hot breath on her face. Suddenly the air was filled with an electronic warbling. At once the roaring of the Myrkas stopped.

Lizzie forced one eye open. The monsters were lumbering away from them. They were heading towards the soldiers again.

'What did you do?' she asked.

The Doctor peered after them. 'I threw a stick for them!'

'I'm sorry?'

'Well, I created a sonic signal that the Myrkas will follow, so they'll do pretty much what I tell them...'

He tailed off. Lizzie followed his gaze to where Pelham was kneeling down alongside Matt's lifeless body.

'Except they were ordered not to kill anyone,' the Doctor went on. 'They were just meant to keep the Navy boys busy. The pain from the heat gun must have driven them mad...'

'It wasn't your fault. You tried to warn him.'

The Doctor nodded and crossed to Pelham's side. 'I'm sorry.'

Pelham said nothing.

In the distance, the Doctor could hear the rattle of machine guns, and the muffled sound of the soldiers as they retreated from the bellowing monsters.

'We really do need to get out of here. The Myrkas will drive everyone out of the area. I can finish this here and now.'

Pelham looked up at the Doctor sadly. 'Matt never questioned me. Never. He really did think that I was right.'

'He was wrong.'

Pelham stiffened. His hand reached out for the Sea Devil heat gun clutched in Matt's lifeless fingers.

The Doctor took a step backwards, pulling Lizzie behind him. 'Mr Pelham. Please. That's not going to help anyone. We can sort this out. I promise you. We can escape.'

The answer came from behind them: 'No, human, there is no escape for any of you.'

The Doctor whirled to find General Veldac glaring at them, hatred in his jet-black eyes.

He was still groggy, swaying unsteadily on his feet, but the flat disc of his heat gun was aimed right at them.

'It's over, General.' The Doctor did his best to stay calm. 'Partock, Oclar and the others are all back in hibernation. The best thing you can do is join them.'

'You lie!'

'Look around you, General. This place is nothing but ice and rock. There is nothing for your people here. Lead your troops back into the sea. Hibernation is your only option.'

'Perhaps you are right, Doctor.' Veldac lowered his weapon. 'But if we cannot reclaim this planet, then at least I can take it from *you*.'

The Sea Devil turned and aimed his weapon at the convoy of tractors loaded with barrels of Fire Ice. 'If Partock was right, there is enough altered fuel here to make this planet unbearable for humans. We will emerge when the Sun has done its work and made this land green once more.'

There was a harsh buzz and a searing blast of heat as Pelham fired the Sea Devil weapon. The ice beneath General Veldac's feet vanished in a cloud of hissing steam, and the Sea Devil commander vanished from view.

'Oh, you beauty!' The Doctor couldn't hide

the astonishment in his voice. 'That's perfect! The heat ray will have scrambled the thermal control on his armour. He'll be thrown into emergency hibernation mode!'

Pelham tossed the heat gun through the smoking hole in the ice. 'Can we get out of here now, please?'

The three of them hurried towards the waiting helicopter. As Pelham clambered into the pilot's seat, he pressed the button on the radio.

'Admiral Turner,' he said. 'Tell your troops to pull out. The base power system is going critical. The explosion will be local, but the shockwave will probably crack the ice sheet. Abandon the barrels. Concentrate on getting the personnel clear.'

The helicopter lifted into the air.

Chapter Fourteen

Pelham's helicopter hovered high over the Antarctic ice. The Doctor watched through the window. He waited until he was certain that the Navy helicopters were also at a safe distance. Then he pressed the trigger button.

The explosion was huge. The centre of the base blew out in a vast ball of flame. Sections of roof and wall were sent spinning high into the cold, grey sky. Seconds later, smaller fireballs started to blow the base apart room by room as the chain reaction speeded up. It was like watching a house of cards topple. Lizzie couldn't believe how fast the destruction spread. The noise from the explosions was like fireworks on Bonfire Night.

A second huge blast rocked the helicopter as the drill-head building blew into a million pieces. The tall tower started to topple, and in seconds it was nothing but burning wreckage on the ice.

For a moment there was silence, and Lizzie thought that it was all over. But suddenly there was a noise like a giant whip being cracked. A massive crack started to spread out across the surface of the ice. Moments later, another split appeared, then another and another. It was like watching a speeded up film. The web of cracks spread and multiplied, forming a vast pattern on the ice.

With the ice sheet fractured, the weight of the base was too much to support. Half the buildings vanished through the ice into the lake below in a cloud of billowing smoke and steam. More and more of the ice started to collapse, spreading out in an ever-widening circle. The convoy of tractors, loaded with barrels of Fire Ice vanished into the lake. Myrkas roared as the ground collapsed beneath them and they were swallowed up by the freezing water.

It was a vision of hell.

As the last remnant of the PelCorp base vanished from view, a plume of steam and embers was thrown, hissing, into the Antarctic sky. When the cloud cleared, there was no sign that the base had ever existed.

The Doctor gazed sadly down at the vast expanse of grey water that had not seen the light of the Sun for millions of years. In time, the ice would reform, sealing off the Silurian base again. The Myrkas and the Sea Devils could only survive if they returned to their hibernation chambers. To sleep once more.

And the Fire Ice...

The Doctor glanced across at the man who claimed that he had discovered it. Somehow the Doctor doubted that he would ever come looking for it again.

Lizzie squeezed the Doctor's arm. 'Is he going to be OK?'

'He'll be fine. In fact you might even think about recruiting him to your cause.'

'You're kidding, right?' she said.

'He's got lots of money,' the Doctor told her. 'Lots of expertise. You could do much worse.'

Lizzie stared at him with a mixture of surprise and admiration. 'You're always going to give people a second chance, aren't you, Doctor?'

The Doctor just smiled, and let the bomb control drop from his fingers. He watched as it was swallowed up by the cold, grey waters below.

Books in the Quick Reads series

Amy's Diary	Maureen Lee
Beyond the Bounty	Tony Parsons
Bloody Valentine	James Patterson
Buster Fleabags	Rolf Harris
Chickenfeed	Minette Walters
Cleanskin	Val McDermid
The Cleverness of Ladies	Alexander McCall Smith
Clouded Vision	Linwood Barclay
A Cool Head	Ian Rankin
The Dare	John Boyne
Doctor Who: Code of the Krillitanes	Justin Richards
Doctor Who: Made of Steel	Terrance Dicks
Doctor Who: Magic of the Angels	Jacqueline Rayner
Doctor Who: Revenge of the Judoon	Terrance Dicks
Doctor Who: The Silurian Gift	Mike Tucker
Doctor Who: The Sontaran Games	Jacqueline Rayner
A Dreadful Murder	Minette Walters
A Dream Come True	Maureen Lee
Follow Me	Sheila O'Flanagan
Full House	Maeve Binchy
Get the Life You Really Want	James Caan
The Grey Man	Andy McNab
Hello Mum	Bernardine Evaristo

How to Change Your Life in 7 Steps	John Bird
Humble Pie	Gordon Ramsay
Jack and Jill	Lucy Cavendish
Kung Fu Trip	Benjamin Zephaniah
Last Night Another Soldier	Andy McNab
Life's New Hurdles	Colin Jackson
Life's Too Short	Val McDermid, Editor
Lily	Adèle Geras
The Little One	Lynda La Plante
Love is Blind	Kathy Lette
Men at Work	Mike Gayle
Money Magic	Alvin Hall
One Good Turn	Chris Ryan
The Perfect Holiday	Cathy Kelly
The Perfect Murder	Peter James
Quantum of Tweed: The Man with the Nissan Micra	Conn Iggulden
RaW Voices: True Stories of Hardship and Hope	Vanessa Feltz
Reading My Arse!	Ricky Tomlinson
A Sea Change	Veronica Henry
Star Sullivan	Maeve Binchy
Strangers on the 16:02	Priya Basil
Survive the Worst and Aim for the Best	Kerry Katona
The 10 Keys to Success	John Bird
Tackling Life	Charlie Oatway
Today Everything Changes	Andy McNab
Traitors of the Tower	Alison Weir
Trouble on the Heath	Terry Jones
Twenty Tales from the War Zone	John Simpson
We Won the Lottery	Danny Buckland
Wrong Time, Wrong Place	Simon Kernick

Start a new chapter

Quick Reads are brilliant short new books by bestselling authors and celebrities. We hope you enjoyed this one!

Find out more at **www.quickreads.org.uk**

 @Quick_Reads   Quick-Reads

We would like to thank all our funders:

LOTTERY FUNDED

We would also like to thank all our partners in the Quick Reads project for their help and support: NIACE, unionlearn, National Book Tokens, The Reading Agency, National Literacy Trust, Welsh Books Council, The Big Plus Scotland, DELNI, NALA

At Quick Reads, World Book Day and World Book Night we want to encourage everyone in the UK and Ireland to read more and discover the joy of books.

World Book Day is on 7 March 2013
Find out more at **www.worldbookday.com**

World Book Night is on 23 April 2013
Find out more at **www.worldbooknight.org**

Doctor Who: I Am a Dalek
Gareth Roberts

BBC Books

Equipped with space suits, golf clubs and a flag, the Doctor and Rose are planning to live it up on the Moon, Apollo-mission style. But the TARDIS has other plans, landing them instead in a village on the south coast of England; a picture-postcard sort of place where nothing much happens...until now.

Archaeologists have dug up a Roman mosaic, dating from the year 70 AD. It shows scenes from ancient myths, bunches of grapes – and a Dalek. A few days later a young woman, rushing to get to work, is knocked over and killed by a bus. Then she comes back to life.

It's not long before all hell breaks loose, and the Doctor and Rose must use all their courage and cunning against an alien enemy – and a not-quite-alien accomplice – who are intent on destroying humanity.

Featuring the Doctor and Rose as played by David Tennant and Billie Piper in the hit series from BBC Television.

Doctor Who: Made of Steel
by Terrance Dicks

BBC Books

A deadly night attack on an army base. Vehicles are destroyed, soldiers killed. The attackers vanish as swiftly as they came, taking highly advanced equipment with them.

Metal figures attack a shopping mall. But why do they only want a new games console from an ordinary electronics shop? An obscure government ministry is blown up – but, in the wreckage, no trace is found of the secret, state-of-the-art decoding equipment.

When the TARDIS returns the Doctor and Martha to Earth from a distant galaxy, they try to piece together the mystery. But someone – or something – is waiting for them. An old enemy stalks the night, men no longer made of flesh…

Featuring the Doctor and Martha as played by David Tennant and Freema Agyeman in the hit series *Doctor Who* from BBC Television.

Doctor Who: Revenge of the Judoon
by Terrance Dicks

BBC Books

The TARDIS brings the Doctor and Martha to Balmoral in 1902. Here they meet Captain Harry Carruthers – friend of the new king, Edward VII. Together they head for the castle to see the King – only to find that Balmoral Castle has gone, leaving just a hole in the ground. The Doctor realises it is the work of the Judoon – a race of ruthless space police.

While Martha and Carruthers seek answers in London, the Doctor finds himself in what should be the most deserted place on Earth – and he is not alone.

With help from Arthur Conan Doyle, the Doctor and his friends discover a plot to take over the world. With time running out, who will fall victim to the revenge of the Judoon?

Featuring the Doctor and Martha as played by David Tennant and Freema Agyeman in the hit series *Doctor Who* from BBC Television.

Doctor Who: The Sontaran Games
Jacqueline Rayner

BBC Books

Every time the lights go out, someone dies…

The TARDIS lands at an academy for top athletes, all hoping to be chosen for the forthcoming Globe Games. But is one of them driven enough to resort to murder? The Doctor discovers that the students have been hushing up unexplained deaths.

Teaming up with a young swimmer called Emma, the Doctor begins to investigate – but he doesn't expect to find a squad of Sontarans invading the academy!

As the Sontarans begin their own lethal version of the Globe Games, the Doctor and Emma must find out what's really going on. But the Doctor is captured and forced to take part in the Sontaran Games. Can even a Time Lord survive this deadly contest?

Featuring the Doctor as played by David Tennant in the acclaimed hit series from BBC Television.

Doctor Who: Code of the Krillitanes
Justin Richards

BBC Books

Can eating a bag of crisps really make you more clever? The company that makes the crisps says so, and they seem to be right.

But the Doctor is worried. Who would want to make people more brainy? And why?

With just his sonic screwdriver and a supermarket trolley full of crisps, the Doctor sets out to find the truth. The answer is scary – the Krillitanes are back on Earth, and everyone is at risk!

Last time they took over a school. This time they have hijacked the internet. Whatever they are up to, it's big and it's nasty.

Only the Doctor can stop them – if he isn't already too late…

Featuring the Doctor as played by David Tennant in the acclaimed hit series from BBC Television.

Doctor Who: Magic of the Angels
Jacqueline Rayner

BBC Books

*'No one from this time
will ever see that girl again…'*

On a sight-seeing tour of London the Doctor wonders why so many young girls are going missing. When he sees Sammy Star's amazing magic act, he thinks he knows the answer. The Doctor and his friends team up with residents of an old people's home to discover the truth. And together they find themselves face to face with a deadly Weeping Angel.

Whatever you do – don't blink!

A thrilling all-new adventure featuring the Doctor, Amy and Rory, as played by Matt Smith, Karen Gillan and Arthur Darvill in the hit series from BBC Television

Why not start a **Quick Reads** reading group?

If you have enjoyed this book, why not share your next Quick Read with friends, colleagues, or neighbours.

A reading group is a great way to get the most out of a book and is easy to arrange. All you need is a group of people, a place to meet and a date and time that works for everyone.

Use the first meeting to decide which book to read first and how the group will operate. Conversation doesn't have to stick rigidly to the book. Here are some suggested themes for discussions:

- How important was the plot?

- What messages are in the book?

- Discuss the characters – were they believable and could you relate to them?

- How important was the setting to the story?

- Are the themes timeless?

- Personal reactions – what did you like or not like about the book?

There is a free toolkit with lots of ideas to help you run a Quick Reads reading group at **www.quickreads.org.uk**

Share your experiences of your group on Twitter @Quick_Reads

For more ideas, offers and groups to join visit Reading Groups for Everyone at **www.readingagency.org.uk/readinggroups**

Other Resources

Enjoy this book?

Find out about all the others at **www.quickreads.org.uk**

For Quick Reads audio clips as well as videos
and ideas to help you enjoy reading visit
www.bbc.co.uk/skillswise

Skillswise

Join the Reading Agency's Six Book Challenge at
www.readingagency.org.uk/sixbookchallenge

**THE
READING
AGENCY**

Find more books for new readers at
www.newisland.ie
www.barringtonstoke.co.uk

Free courses to develop your skills are available in your
local area. To find out more phone 0800 100 900.

For more information on developing your skills
in Scotland visit **www.thebigplus.com**

Want to read more? Join your local library. You can borrow
books for free and take part in inspiring reading activities.